THE MISSING KITTEN

THE MISSING KITTEN

Holly Webb

Illustrated by Sophy Williams

First published in Great Britain in 2013
by Stripes Publishing
an imprint of Little Tiger Press
This Large Print edition published 2013
by AudioGO Ltd
by arrangement with
Stripes Publishing
an imprint of Little Tiger Press

ISBN: 978 1471 354571

British Library Cataloguing in Publication Data available

Printed and bound in Great Britain by
TJ International Limited

For Emily and the gorgeous
Rosie Bumble

CHAPTER ONE

Scarlett looked around her new bedroom with delight. It was huge! And as it was up in the roof of the cottage, it was a really interesting shape, all ups and downs. There was a gorgeous window as well, with a curly handle to open it, and a big, wide windowsill she could sit on. Her old bedroom had been tiny, and a very boring squarish sort of shape.

'Good, isn't it?' Jackson, her big brother, put his head round the door. He had the bedroom next to hers, which was basically the other half of the roof space. Mum and Dad had said that their bedrooms used to be the attic.

'I love it,' Scarlett said happily. 'The window's the best thing! I love seeing all the fields and trees, and look! Cows! Out of my bedroom window!'

Jackson chuckled. 'Cows not cars. Now *that* makes a change! Yeah, it's really good. Except everything's a bit far away.'

Scarlett nodded slowly. 'There *is* a shop in the village,' she reminded him.

Jackson made a face. 'Yeah, one shop! And a blacksmith. How weird is that?'

'And the school's in the village too,' Scarlett added, very quietly. 'I wish we didn't have to change schools.' That was the thing she was least happy about with their move to the countryside. She was really going to miss her old school, and her friends. Lucy and Ella had said they'd come and stay in the next holidays, but that was a long time away. And meanwhile, she was going to start at a school where she didn't know anyone, and she certainly didn't have any friends.

'It'll be all right,' Jackson told her cheerfully, and Scarlett sighed. He wasn't worried. He never was. Jackson was really sporty, and he found it very easy to make friends. And yet he didn't show off, so people just wanted to hang out with him. Scarlett wished she knew how he did it.

'Did you hear that rustling noise?' Jackson pointed up at the ceiling. 'I bet there are mice in all that thatch. Remember to tell Mum and Dad about that, Scarlett. You need to start working on them again about a kitten, now that we're here. They said maybe after we'd moved, didn't they?'

Scarlett grinned at him. 'I know! I thought I'd maybe give them a day though, before I started asking. Let them get some boxes unpacked first . . .' She looked up too. 'Do you really think there are mice?'

Jackson gazed thoughtfully at the ceiling. 'Probably. It sounds like it to me. Unless it's a rat, of course.'

'Uuurgh! OK, I'll ask Mum now. No way am I living in a house with a rat!' Scarlett shuddered.

'I'm with you on that,' Jackson grinned. 'Rats can be pretty big, you know. Bigger than a kitten, anyway.' He made a ratty face, pulling his lips back to show big ratty teeth.

'Stop it!' Scarlett cried. 'Maybe we can get a grown-up cat then. I don't mind if it isn't a little kitten. I'd just love to have any sort of cat, and they did say maybe we could. You'll help, won't you? You'll ask too?'

Jackson nodded. 'Yeah. Although I don't fancy coming down in the morning to find a row of dead mice on the doormat. That's what Sam says his cat does.'

Scarlett looked worried. 'I think I'd rather have a cat that just scares the mice away . . .'

Scarlett started her kitten campaign while everyone was sitting down eating lunch. It felt really odd seeing their old kitchen table in a completely different kitchen.

'It's so quiet,' Mum said happily,

4

looking out of the open window. 'I don't think I've heard a single car since we got here. I love it that we're down at the end of the lane.'

'I keep thinking there's something missing,' Dad admitted. 'But it'll be great once we're used to it. And the air smells amazing.'

Jackson sniffed loudly. 'That's cowpat, Dad.'

Scarlett made a face at him. She didn't want him distracting Mum and Dad—this was a great opportunity to mention a kitten. She took a deep

5

breath. 'It's not a bit like Laurence Road, is it?' she said, thinking about their old home. 'With all the busy traffic . . .' She swallowed, and glanced hopefully from Mum to Dad and back again. 'You wouldn't worry about a cat getting run over here, would you?'

Dad snorted with laughter and turned to Mum. 'You win, Laura. She lasted more than an hour.'

Scarlett blinked. 'What do you mean?'

Mum reached out an arm and hugged her round the shoulder. 'Dad and I were talking about it last night, Scarlett. We wondered how long you'd be able to wait before you asked about a cat. I said that I thought it would be once we'd settled in a bit, and Dad said you'd ask the moment we got here. So I won, and now he has to cook dinner tonight!'

'Simple. Fish and chips,' Dad said, taking a huge bite of sandwich.

Mum smiled at him. 'You do realize it's a twenty-minute drive to the nearest fish and chip shop now, don't you?'

'You mean you were just waiting for me to ask? So can we have one?' Scarlett said hopefully, eager to get back to talking about kittens.

Mum nodded slowly. 'Yes. But we can't go off to an animal shelter tomorrow—we need to do some unpacking, and besides, I haven't a clue where the nearest one is.'

'I could find out!' Scarlett said eagerly. 'It's just—it would be really nice to have time to get to know the kitten before school starts. We've only got two weeks, and then me and Jackson won't be at home for most of the day.'

Dad nodded. 'I know, Scarlett, but I don't think we'll be able to find you a kitten right now. I know it would be lovely to have one while you're still at home. But it won't be a huge problem if you're at school. Mum'll be at work, but I'll be at home working, so the kitten won't be lonely. And your new school's really close. You'll be home in ten minutes.'

Scarlett nodded. That was another thing that was different, being able to

7

walk to school. Mum and Dad had even said she and Jackson could walk on their own, if they wanted, as it was all along footpaths.

'I suppose.' Scarlett nodded. 'So we can really have a cat? You actually mean it? We can look for one?'

'Promise,' Dad told her solemnly.

Scarlett beamed at him. She could come home from school and play with her cat. Her own cat! She'd wanted to have one for so long, and now it was going to happen.

'Scarlett! I'm off to the village,' Dad yelled up the stairs.

Scarlett shoved an armful of T-shirts into the drawer, and dashed out of her room. 'I'm coming!'

She really wanted to walk there. They'd seen the village a couple of times before. The first time was when they came to look at the house. Mum had got her new job at the hospital, and Mum and Dad explained that they would need to move, as it was too far for her to drive every day. Scarlett had really missed her for those few weeks when she'd been leaving early, and not getting back until it was almost time for Scarlett to go to bed. Now they'd moved, the hospital was only half an hour away, in Leaming, the nearest big town to their tiny little village, which was called Leaming Ford. Once they'd made the decision that Mum would take the job, and agreed to buy the cottage, Scarlett and Jackson had gone for a day's visit at their new school, and seen the village again. But Scarlett had been so nervous about the school, she couldn't remember what it was like.

'It's so pretty,' she murmured, as they walked along the footpath. 'Look at all the flowers. I saw a rabbit last night, Dad, did I tell you?'

'Only about six times! I nearly had a heart attack when you screamed like that. I thought you'd fallen out of the window.'

'Sorry! I was excited! I've never seen a rabbit in my garden before!' Scarlett giggled. 'Can we go down here? Is it the right way?'

Dad nodded. 'Yup, this is the quickest path down to the village, the way you and Jackson will go to school, probably.'

Scarlett swallowed nervously. She was still worrying about the school. It was tiny, which was nice, she supposed. There wouldn't be that many people to get to know. But they'd probably all been together since playgroup. They might not want a stranger joining their class at all.

Dad nudged her gently with his elbow. 'You had a good time on your visit, didn't you?'

Scarlett looked up at him, surprised.

'It was pretty obvious what you were thinking, sweetheart.'

'I suppose. Yes. Everyone was nice. But that was just one morning. I've got to go there every day . . .'

'It'll be great. You'll be fine, I'm sure you will.'

Scarlett nodded. She didn't really want to think about it. 'Look—is that the village? I can see houses.' She ran on ahead. 'And there's the shop, Dad, look.'

10

'I'd better find the list,' Dad muttered, searching his pockets. 'We definitely need bread. Can you be in charge of finding that for me? Now where on earth did I put it?'

But Scarlett wasn't listening. She had seen something—a noticeboard in the shop window. It was full of advertisements—exercise classes in the church hall, someone offering to make celebration cakes, a nearly new lawnmower for sale . . .

And a litter of kittens, three black-and-white, one ginger, ready to leave their mother now, free to good homes.

CHAPTER TWO

'Dad! Look!' Scarlett was so excited, she couldn't keep still—she was dancing from foot to foot, pointing madly at the notice.

'What?' Her dad hurried up, peering into the window. 'Oh! I can see why you're so excited. 'Ready now', hmmm?' He read the advert through thoughtfully, and then got his phone out.

'Are you going to call them?' Scarlett squeaked excitedly.

'No. I'm going to put the number into my phone, get some bread and milk, and go home and talk it over with your mother. Can you imagine what she'd say if we went out for shopping and came home with a kitten?'

Scarlett sighed. 'I suppose you're right. It would be funny though.' She giggled. "Hi, Mum, here's the milk . . ." And we take a kitten out of the bag!'

'It might have been here a while, this notice,' Dad pointed out. 'The kittens might all have gone. Don't get your hopes up, OK?'

Scarlett nodded. But as they paid for the shopping, she took a deep breath and smiled at the lady behind the counter. She hated talking to people she didn't know, but this was important. 'Excuse me, but you see the notice in the window about the kittens? Has it been up for long—I mean, do you know if they still have any left?'

The lady beamed at her. 'After a kitten, are you? Julie Mallins will be pleased. She only put the notice up earlier this week, and I know she's still looking for homes for them all.'

'Really?' Scarlett was dancing around again, she just couldn't help it. 'Oh Dad, can we go home and talk to Mum

14

about it now, please?'

'All right, all right!' Dad grinned, raising his eyebrows at the lady.

Scarlett ran all the way home—in fact, she went twice as far as Dad did, because he wouldn't run too, so she kept having to turn round and run all the way back to him to tell him to hurry up. When she raced in through the front of the cottage, she was completely out of breath.

'Mum! Mum!' she gasped, running from the living room to the kitchen and back to the bottom of the stairs.

'What's the matter, sweetheart?' Her mum backed out of the understairs cupboard, where she'd been putting coats and wellies away. 'Scarlett, you're scarlet!' It was an old family joke.

'Ha ha. Mum, there's someone in the village who's got a litter of kittens they want to give away!'

'Really?'

'There was a notice up in the village shop.' Dad came in, holding out his phone. 'I've got the number, what do you think?'

Scarlett bit her lip to stop herself shrieking 'please, please, please'. Her mum was very firm about not whining, and she really didn't want to get on the wrong side of her right now.

'Well, I suppose we could ask to go and look at them . . .' her mum said, rather doubtfully. 'I'm just a bit worried that the house is all upside down right now while we're still unpacking. Wouldn't that be stressful for a kitten?'

Scarlett's face fell. Mum was right. 'Maybe we could wait?' she whispered.

16

'Maybe we could just choose a kitten and ask them to keep it for us a bit longer?' She really wanted to have a kitten now, but she didn't want their new pet to start out scared by all the boxes everywhere.

Dad hugged her. 'Well, let's see what Julie says—that's the owner,' he explained to Mum. 'She might not think it's a problem. To be honest, we've done most of the unpacking in the kitchen already. We could keep it in there for the time being—I think you have to keep new kittens in one room to start off with anyway.'

Mum nodded. 'I'd forgotten that. We used to have a cat when I was little,' she told Scarlett, 'but it's ever such a long time ago. We'll all have to learn how to look after a cat together.'

'What?' Jackson put his head round the kitchen door. 'Are we getting one? What's happening?'

'Scarlett found a notice about a litter of kittens needing homes,' Dad told him. 'We should have known—if there were kittens around, Scarlett was bound to find them! Shall I call this lady then?'

Mum nodded, and Scarlett flung her arms around her. She held her breath and listened as Dad made the phone call.

'Hi, is that Julie? We saw your advert about the kittens . . . Mmm . . . We wondered if we'd be able to come and see them? Uh-huh. Well, now's great, if that's really OK with you. Fantastic. Kendall's Lane. Oh, off the main road? See you in about ten minutes then.'

Scarlett gasped. Ten minutes! Ten minutes till they saw their kitten!

'Here they are.'

Julie turned out to be a really sweet lady, who'd adopted Goldie, the kittens' mum, after finding her eating scraps of bread under her bird table,

18

because she was a stray, and so terribly hungry.

'It took weeks to even get her to come inside,' Julie told Scarlett, as she led them through to the kitchen. 'But she's settling down now. I think she knew she needed to let someone look after her, so she could have her kittens somewhere nice and warm.'

'How old are the kittens?' Scarlett's mum asked as Julie opened the kitchen door.

'Ten weeks—the vet said they should be fine to go to new homes,' Scarlett heard Julie say. But she wasn't really concentrating. Instead, she was staring at the basket in the corner, where a beautiful brownish tabby cat was curled up, with four kittens mounded around and on top of her.

'Goodness, she looks tired,' Mum murmured.

'Yes, I think she is, poor thing. She's been a really good mum, but she was so thin to start with, apart from her huge tummy full of kittens. I was worried that she wouldn't be able to feed them, but she's done very well. They're all

19

practically weaned now—they love their food!'

Woken by the voices, one of the kittens popped his head up, his big gingery ears twitching with interest.

'Oh, look at him!' Scarlett whispered. 'His ears are too big for him!'

Julie nodded. 'I know, he's cute, isn't he? He's got massive paws too; I think he's going to be a really big cat.'

The kitten gently biffed the brother or sister next to him with the side of his chin, and the rest of the kittens popped up in a line, staring at Scarlett and Jackson.

20

The other three were black and white, very pretty, without the massive ears. They had enormous whiskers instead—great big white moustaches of them.

'I like the ginger one,' Jackson said. 'That one's a boy, right?'

Julie nodded. 'Yes, and the three black and white ones are all girls.'

'I like him too,' Scarlett agreed. 'Will they let us stroke them? Is that OK?'

'They're usually very friendly. Especially Ginger.'

'Oh, is that what he's called?' Scarlett tried not to sound disappointed. She would have liked to choose a name together for their kitten—Ginger was what all ginger cats were called!

'Oh no. I've tried not to give them names—I'm hoping to find homes for them all, and if I name them I'll just want to keep them. But it's hard not to think of him as Ginger.'

The ginger kitten was standing up now, arching his back and stretching as he climbed out of the basket. He looked sideways at Scarlett with his big blue eyes, to check that she was

admiring how handsome he was as he
stretched. She was watching him
eagerly, and she gave a little sigh of
delight as he stepped towards her,
gently rubbing himself against her arm.

'Oh, he's got boots!' Scarlett looked
over at Jackson and her mum and dad.
'Look, he's got furry white boots on!'

Mum laughed. 'He does look like he
has,' she agreed. 'Those are very cute.'

'I know lots of cats have white paws,
but I've never seen one where the
white goes that far up before.' Scarlett
stroked the ginger kitten lovingly, and
his black and white sisters followed him

22

out of the basket, looking for some attention too. Their mother stared watchfully after them, then seemed to decide that Scarlett and the others weren't dangerous to her babies. She gave a massive yawn, and curled up for a sleep.

The girl kittens let Scarlett's mum and dad pet them, then they set off chasing after a feathery cat toy, racing round the kitchen and patting it ahead of them with their paws. The ginger kitten watched them, but he didn't join in. Instead he placed a hopeful paw on Scarlett's knee, and she looked back at him, just as hopefully. Did he want to be picked up?

'He's very cuddly,' Julie said quietly. 'He's a real people cat. Try and put him on your lap.'

Scarlett gently wrapped her hands around his gingery middle. Even though he was the biggest of the kittens, he still felt tiny—so light, as though there was nothing to him.

The kitten gave a pleased little squeak, and padded his fat white paws up and down her jeans as though he

23

was testing how comfy she was. Scarlett found herself smoothing her jeans, wanting him to think she was nice to sit on. He padded all the way round in a circle a couple of times, and then wobbled and flopped down, stretching his front paws out, and flexing his claws gently in and out of the denim fabric of her jeans.

'That tickles!' Scarlett giggled, stroking him under his little white chin.

The kitten purred delightedly. That was the best place, the spot he was always itchy. He pointed his chin to the ceiling and purred louder, telling her to keep going.

Jackson joined in, stroking one finger gently down the kitten's back. 'His fur's really soft. And look at his paws! They're bright pink underneath!' The kitten was enjoying the stroking so much that he'd collapsed into a happy heap on his side, purring like a steam train.

Scarlett looked down at his paws and laughed—they really were pink. A sort of pinkish-apricot colour, and so soft and smooth-looking.

'They'll probably get a bit darker once he starts going outside,' Julie explained. 'They've only been indoors so far. He'd need to stay in for a bit longer if you decide to take him.' She looked at Scarlett's mum and dad.

Scarlett and Jackson got up, then both turned to look at them too, and their mum laughed. She turned to Julie, and asked hopefully, 'I don't suppose you could lend us some cat litter, could you? The shop in the village would have cat food . . .'

'You mean we can take him now?' Scarlett gasped.

Her mum shrugged. 'Why not?'

CHAPTER THREE

'Dad, we're nearly out of Bootle's food. There's only the salmon flavour left, and I don't think he liked that one very much.'

Bootle wrapped himself lovingly round Scarlett's legs. He knew quite well what was in those tins, and he didn't see any reason why he shouldn't have a second breakfast.

Calling him Bootle had been Jackson's idea. Scarlett had suggested Boots, but it was like Ginger—a little bit too everyday for such a special cat. Bootle was much better.

Jackson looked up from his huge pile

of toast. 'We could go to the shop,' he said. 'I've nearly finished the bread, and there's not a lot for lunch.'

'I've got a work call in a few minutes,' said Dad. He looked at them thoughtfully. 'Though I suppose you guys could go if you like.'

'On our own?' Scarlett stared at him.

'Why not? You were going to try it when school started next week, weren't you? If you're careful, and you stick together.'

Scarlett shut her eyes for a second at the mention of school. She was trying not to think about it. 'Will you look after Bootle while we're out?' she said seriously.

'Scarlett! You'll only be gone half an hour!' Dad grinned.

'But he's not used to me not being here!' It was true. Scarlett had spent all of her time with Bootle since they'd brought him home, only leaving him at night-time, when he was safely tucked up in his cardboard box, padded out with an old towel, and a hot water bottle to feel like his mother and the other kittens. Just until he got used to them not being next to him.

'I think it would be good for him to see you go out,' her dad said gently. 'I know you don't want to think about school, Scarlett, but you do go on Monday. Bootle's had a whole week of you around all the time. He needs to learn to be without you.'

'But he'll be lonely,' Scarlett said worriedly.

'It's only for half an hour,' Dad reminded her.

'When we're back at school it won't be!'

'Then he'll have me for company while I'm working. And you know how he loves the computer.'

Scarlett smiled. It was true. Bootle was fascinated by Dad's computer. He seemed to love the way the keys went up and down. He would sit watching Dad type for ages, just occasionally putting out a paw to try and join in. Then he would look miffed when Dad told him no. Secretly Scarlett was planning to let him try one day when she was using the laptop she shared with Jackson. She wanted to see what

Bootle would write—she knew it would probably be a string of random letters, but she was hoping for a secret message!

'Come on then.' Jackson stuffed the last of the toast into his mouth. 'Can we get some crisps as well while we're at the shop, Dad?'

'Mmm-hmm. Here.' Dad gave Jackson some money. 'But I do want change. Be back by half-ten, all right? I don't want to be pacing up and down outside looking for you.'

'Are you really worried about school?' Jackson asked Scarlett, as they wandered down the footpath in the direction of the village.

'A bit.' Scarlett sighed. 'What if nobody talks to me?'

'Why wouldn't they?' Jackson asked, shrugging.

Scarlett shook her head. He was trying to be nice, but he just didn't get it.

'You had loads of friends at your old

school,' said Jackson. 'Why do you think you won't make friends here?'

'It's such a little school,' Scarlett tried to explain. 'Only one class in each year, and not that many in each class, either. They'll all know each other so well. Like I know Lucy and Ella.' She wished she was as confident as Jackson. He'd already managed to go out for a walk and found a couple of boys playing football. He'd joined in, and then he'd gone back to their house. Scarlett wasn't sure how he did it.

Jackson rolled his eyes. 'Come on. We're nearly there.'

They went into the shop, and Jackson went to look at football magazines, while Scarlett found the cat food. Then she realized that there were a couple of other girls standing behind her.

'Who's she?' one of them whispered.

'Don't you remember? It's that new girl. The one who came to school for a morning.'

'Ohhh! What's she called?'

'Something weird. Amber or something.'

Scarlett felt like her stomach was

squeezing into a tiny little knot inside her. That was her they were talking about. The one with the weird name. She wanted to scream, 'Scarlett!' But she didn't. She grabbed a couple of tins of cat food, and scuttled over to where Jackson was.

School was going to be a disaster. It was so obvious.

Scarlett lay in bed, watching her clock creep closer to seven. She'd been awake for ages, worrying about their first day at school, and now she just wished it would hurry up and be time.

A throaty purr distracted her, and a soft paw patted her chin. Bootle liked her to be paying attention to him, not the clock.

'I'm glad I went downstairs and fetched you before breakfast,' Scarlett said, tickling him behind the ears. 'I know I look miserable, but you're making me feel a lot better.'

Bootle closed his eyes happily, and purred even louder. Scarlett knew all the places he liked to be stroked, and how he particularly liked being on her bed. It was much cosier than his basket.

'I'm really going to miss you today,' Scarlett murmured. 'I hope you'll be OK. Dad'll look after you.' She sighed, a huge sigh that lifted up the duvet round her middle, and Bootle's ears twitched excitedly. He wriggled forward, and peered down under the duvet. It was like a dark little nest, and

he wriggled into it, just his tail sticking
out, and flicking from side to side.

'What are you doing?' Scarlett
giggled. 'Silly cat! Oh, Bootle, you're
tickling my legs!'

Even the tail had disappeared now.
Bootle was a plump little mound
travelling around under the duvet.
Then he popped out at the other end
of the bed, his ginger fur looking all

spiky and ruffled up. He shook himself, and ran a paw over his ears.

Scarlett twitched her toes under the duvet, and he stopped washing and pounced on them excitedly, jumping from side to side as she wriggled them about.

'You're awake!' Mum put her head round the door. 'Time to get up, Scarlett. Hello, Bootle.' She came in and patted him. 'Are you worried he'll miss you while you're at school?'

Scarlett nodded, and Mum hugged her. 'It'll be fine, sweetheart. Now he's allowed in the garden he'll probably just go out and try and chase butterflies again.' She looked at Scarlett. 'And you'll be fine too. Honestly. Try not to worry about it.'

Scarlett nodded. But she wished she felt as sure as everybody else seemed to.

Bootle sat on the back doorstep, next to his cat flap, staring around the garden. He was confused, and a bit bored. Scarlett had gone somewhere. He'd known that she was going—she had picked him up and made a huge fuss of him before she went, and her voice had been different to normal, as

t h o u g h something was wrong. But he h a d n ' t expected her to be gone this long.

He stalked crossly down the garden, sniffing at the grass, looking for something i n t e r e s t i n g to do. He sharpened his claws on the trunk of the apple tree, and tried to climb it, but he wasn't all that good at climbing yet, and he only got halfway up before he got worried and jumped down again. Then he had to sit and wash for a while, pretending to himself that he'd never meant to climb it in the first place.

Where was she? Jackson had gone too—he preferred to play with Scarlett, but Jackson was very good at inventing games with sticks, and bits of string to jump at.

Why had they gone away and left him? And when were they coming back?

CHAPTER FOUR

'Bootle! Did you miss me?' Scarlett picked him up, and hugged him lovingly, and Bootle rubbed his head against her cheek.

Dad had come to meet them from school, as it was the first day, but tomorrow they were going to walk there and back by themselves.

'Come and have a biscuit,' Dad suggested. 'Then you can both tell me what it was like, now there's no one else around.' When he'd asked Scarlett at the school gate how her day was, she'd just muttered, 'Fine,' but he could tell she was only being polite.

'It was all right.' Jackson shrugged, munching a chocolate biscuit. 'Played football at lunch. The teacher was a bit strict. Shouted at people for talking. But it was fine.'

Dad looked over at Scarlett, who sighed. 'It was OK. This girl called Izzy got told to look after me, and she was nice. She took me around with her at break and lunchtime. But—well, it was only because she had to.'

'She might really like you!' Dad pointed out.

Scarlett ran one of Bootle's huge ears between her fingers, and sighed. 'Maybe . . . It wasn't as bad as it could have been,' she admitted. The two girls she'd seen in the shop hadn't said anything else about her weird name, which was what she'd been worrying about. They'd been on the same table as her and Izzy at lunch, and they'd been quite friendly, and asked her where she lived, and if she'd had to catch the bus to school. It turned out that lots of the children did—they came from several different villages, and a school bus went round and picked them all up.

'It's nice we can walk to school,' she said to Dad, who was still looking worried about her.

Bootle rubbed himself against her red sweater, leaving gingery hairs all over it, and Scarlett stroked him again. Whatever happened at school, at least she could come home and play with him. She couldn't imagine being without him now.

'You're sure you wouldn't like me to come with you?' Dad asked, for about the fourth time.

'No!' Jackson said. 'Honestly, Dad. We're fine. It takes about ten minutes to get to school, and we don't even have to cross a road. Stop fussing.'

Bootle was sitting on the bottom step of the stairs, watching disapprovingly as Scarlett and Jackson got ready. They were going again, just like yesterday! Why was he being left behind? He let out a tiny, furious mew, but Scarlett only kissed the top of his head, and went out of the door, leaving him with Dad.

Dad picked Bootle up, and tickled his ears, before rubbing the top of his head. But then he put him back down on the stairs, and headed into the room where his computer was. He was going to be too busy to play, again.

Bootle stalked into the kitchen, and inspected his food bowl, which was empty. He had a little water, and looked at his basket. He didn't really feel like sleeping. And if this was anything like yesterday, Scarlett and Jackson would be gone for hours.

He didn't see why he couldn't go with them. Until yesterday, he'd been with Scarlett almost all the time.

Bootle walked over to the cat flap and sniffed at it, carefully. They hadn't been gone long. Perhaps, if he was quick, he could follow them. Bootle shot out of the cat flap, and dashed into the back garden. Scarlett and Jackson had gone out of the front door, so he hurried around the side of the house, and on to the little patch of front garden. He nosed his way under the blue gate, flattening himself down underneath the wooden panels, and

coming out into the lane, next to the car. His whiskers twitched excitedly as he tried to work out which way Scarlett had gone. He could follow her scent, he was sure. He sniffed busily at the grasses, and set off running.

Scarlett and Jackson were halfway to school, walking down the footpath along the side of the big field, which was planted with green wheat—Scarlett hadn't known what it was, but Dad had told her.

'Can you hear a meow?' Scarlett asked suddenly, and Jackson turned round to stare at her.

'Don't be silly. Come on!'

'No, I can. I really can. It's Bootle, I'm sure.' Scarlett peered along the track behind them, and laughed. 'It is! Look!'

Bootle was running after them, mewing happily, and as Scarlett crouched down to say hello, he clambered up into her lap and sat there, purring wearily. He'd had to run

faster than he'd ever done before to catch them up.

'What's he doing here?' Jackson shook his head. 'Yes, you're very clever, Bootle,' he admitted, running one hand down the little ginger kitten's back. 'But now we have to take you back home, and we're going to be late.'

'Oh, do we have to take him back?' Scarlett said sadly.

Jackson rolled his eyes. 'Yes, of course we do! We can't take a cat to school, Scarlett!'

'I suppose so.'

'And we have to run, because we're going to be late.'

Scarlett swallowed anxiously. She didn't want to be late, to have to go in after everyone else, and explain what had happened. They hurried back down the footpath and across the lane before bursting through the front door.

Dad came out of his office, looking worried. 'What's happened? Why are you back? I knew I should have gone with you!'

'Don't worry, Dad. It's fine.' Scarlett held out her arms, full of purring ginger kitten. 'Bootle just followed us. He caught up with us as we were going past the big field—the one with wheat in it. We had to bring him back.' She put Bootle into Dad's arms, and he stopped purring and glared at her. He'd gone to find her, and brought her back, and now she was going again!

'Sorry, Bootle. I'd much rather stay with you.' Scarlett stroked his head as

46

she went to leave.

'Come on, Scarlett,' Jackson yelled from the door.

'You'd better run, sweetheart,' Dad said. 'I'd drive you, but by the time we've gone all round by the road, it's longer than the short cut. I'll ring the school and explain why you'll be a bit late, don't worry.'

'Thanks, Dad,' said Scarlett.

When Scarlett and Jackson hurried into the playground, the head, Miss Wilson, was standing at the main door watching out for them.

Scarlett was worried. Luckily, Miss Wilson didn't look cross. She just smiled at them as they raced towards her, and patted Jackson's shoulder. 'Don't worry. I used to have a dog that followed me to school. Still, I've never heard of a cat doing it. He must be very fond of you.'

Scarlett nodded proudly. She hadn't really thought of it like that.

'I've explained to your teachers, so just slip quietly into your classes, all right?'

'Thanks, Miss Wilson.' Scarlett crept,

mouse-like, along the corridor. It was all very well to say to slip in quietly, but everyone was still going to turn and stare at her. She eased open the door of her classroom, wincing as it creaked.

But her teacher, Mrs Mason, just smiled at her, and waved her over to her table, and went on pointing out something on the whiteboard.

'I wondered where you were!' Izzy whispered to her. 'I thought you might not be coming back!'

'It wasn't that bad yesterday,' Scarlett muttered.

'Are you OK?' said Izzy. 'Did you oversleep?'

Scarlett shook her head. 'No. It sounds really stupid, but I had to take my kitten home. He followed us to school.'

'Your kitten did?' Izzy stared at her. 'Oh, I didn't know you had a kitten! I've got a cat. He's called Olly. But he's never followed me anywhere! He's far too lazy. What's your kitten called?'

'Bootle.' Scarlett smiled proudly. 'We've only had him two weeks, and he isn't used to us leaving him. Mrs Mason's giving us a look. I'll tell you more at break, OK?'

Izzy grinned. 'You're so lucky having a kitten.'

Scarlett nodded, and stared at the whiteboard. Izzy was right, she realized. She really was lucky.

CHAPTER FIVE

'I'll keep Bootle inside until after you've gone,' Dad said at breakfast the following morning. 'If I don't open the cat flap for an hour or so, and I pay him lots of attention, I'm sure he'll stay put.'

'I hope so,' said Mum anxiously. 'We don't want him to wander too far. If he starts going out in the lane and along the footpaths, he could easily get lost.' She glanced up at the clock. 'I'd better get going. Have a lovely day, all of you. Scarlett, do you want to invite that nice girl from your class round after school one day? What was she called? Izzy? I can call her mum. She could come tomorrow, perhaps.'

Dad nodded. 'I can pick you all up from school.'

Scarlett smiled. Dad had been so pleased when she'd come home the day before and said she'd actually had a good day at school. She would really like Izzy to come over.

'I'll ask her,' she agreed, tickling Bootle behind the ears. He was sitting on her lap, hoping for bits of toast. He particularly liked toast with Marmite, so Scarlett made sure she always had Marmite on at least one piece now. She tore off a little corner, and passed it down to him, watching him crunch it up and lick at his whiskers for crumbs.

'Do you really think Bootle will be all right?' she asked Dad anxiously. 'I don't want him to be lonely.'

A cautious paw reached up on to the table, aiming for more toast, and Dad snorted. 'He'll be fine. He knows how to look after himself very well. Don't you?' he added, scratching Bootle under his little white chin. 'Yes, you're very lovely. Even if you are trying to

steal yourself a second breakfast.'

Bootle drooped his whiskers, and stared at Dad, his blue eyes round and solemn.

Scarlett giggled. Bootle made it look as though he was starving to death and even Dad was almost convinced. He glanced down at his own plate of toast, and then shook his head firmly.

'That kitten is a shameless liar,' he told Scarlett.

Bootle prowled up and down the hallway, his tail twitching crossly. Scarlett had left him behind again, and now his cat flap was closed. He didn't understand what was happening. Why did she have to keep going away?

'Hey! Bootle! Cat crunchies!' Scarlett's dad came out of the kitchen with a foil packet, and Bootle turned round hopefully. He loved those crunchies, especially the fishy-flavoured ones. 'Good boy. Yes, Scarlett said some of these might cheer you up.'

Bootle laid his ears back as he heard Scarlett's name, and stopped licking the crunchies up out of Dad's hand. Scarlett! Was she about to come back? He looked at Dad hopefully.

'Oh dear. You really do miss her, don't you?' Dad eyed him worriedly. 'She'll be back later, Bootle, I promise. Come on, yummy fish things.'

Bootle ate the rest of the crunchies, but rather slowly. He liked them, but he would have liked them much more if Scarlett had fed them to him. She had a game where she held them in front of his nose, one at a time, and he stretched up to reach. They didn't taste the same out of Dad's hand.

'Good boy, Bootle.' Dad picked him up gently, took him into the office, and put him down on an old armchair. 'Why don't you have a sleep?'

Bootle walked round and round the seat of the chair, stamping his paws into the cushions, till eventually he slumped down and stared gloomily at the door. He didn't feel like sleeping, but he couldn't think of anything else to do.

Bootle sat in front of the cat flap, staring at it hopefully, and uttering plaintive little mews. It was still locked. He knew because he'd tried it, over and over, scrabbling at the door with his claws. But it just wouldn't open.

'Do you need to go out?' Dad asked, coming into the kitchen, and looking at him, concerned. He crouched down next to Bootle, who gave his knee a hopeful nudge. 'I suppose it can't hurt, it's more than an hour since Jackson and Scarlett left for school.' Dad turned the catch on the cat flap and pushed it, showing Bootle that it was open. 'Off you go.'

Bootle mewed gratefully, and wriggled through the cat flap, trotting purposefully out into the back garden, and straight round to the front of the house, just as he'd done the day before. Next, he was squeezing under the gate, and out into the lane. This time he didn't run as fast. He knew that he'd been shut in the house a long time, and he wouldn't be able to chase Scarlett the way he had the day before.

So he padded down the path, sniffing thoughtfully here and there. It was difficult to follow the traces of Scarlett and Jackson—the cottage smelled of them too, much more than the path, which made it confusing. But he was pretty sure they'd gone this way. Bootle bounded happily along, hoping that they would be in the field again, perhaps sitting down, waiting for him.

But no one was there. Bootle walked

up and down the edge of the huge field, staring anxiously into the green stalks. Was Scarlett in there? She might be, but he couldn't smell her, or hear her. He slipped in between two rows of wheat, pushing his way through the green stalks, and mewing.

Then his ears twitched. There was a scuffling noise ahead of him, and a small bird fluttered out of the wheat, making Bootle leap back in surprise.

He'd seen birds in the garden, but never up close. He hissed at it crossly, but the bird was already half-hopping, half-flying away. Bootle followed it sadly out of the wheat stalks. He didn't think Scarlett was here.

Glancing around the narrow path at the edge of the field, he tried to remember what Scarlett had been doing when he ran after her yesterday. They had been walking along here, away from him, as though they were making for the hedge at the end of the field.

Determinedly, Bootle padded along,

hopping over the ruts and big clumps of grass, and keeping a hopeful eye out for Scarlett. At the corner of the field there was a gap in the hedge, and then a short muddy lane, leading out on to a road with a pavement. Bootle had never really seen a road, and he jumped back, his whiskers bristling, as a car roared past. He had been in a car when he left his mum to come to Scarlett's house, and then when he'd had to go to the vet for his vaccinations, but both times he had been in a basket. From kitten height, the cars going along the road were enormous, and terrifyingly noisy.

He crept into the muddy lane, eyeing the opening out on to the pavement. His ears were laid nervously back, but at the same time Bootle breathed out the faintest little purr. The cars weren't the only noise he could hear. There was shouting, and laughter—the sort of noises Scarlett and Jackson made. He wasn't sure it was them, but it was worth looking. The sounds were coming from very close by. If he was brave enough to go out on to the pavement, close to those cars, he was sure he could find the place.

Bootle dashed out, scurrying along low to the ground, and pressing as far into the hedge as he could go. Every time a car went past—which wasn't very often, thankfully—he buried himself under the prickly, twiggy bits at the bottom of the hedge, and peered out, his blue eyes round and fearful.

The school was only a couple of hundred metres along the main road through the village, and on the same side as the lane. Bootle squirmed under the metal fence at the side of the playground, and scuttled behind a wooden bench, where he sat, curled up as small as he could, and watched the children racing around the tarmac square.

It was very noisy. He had thought Scarlett and Jackson were loud, but there were so many children here. And they were all wearing the same red cardigans and grey skirts, or shorts. He couldn't see Scarlett at all.

He shrank back behind the bench as

a loud bell shrilled, and the children streamed back into the building on the far side of the playground. Then his ears pricked up, and he darted forward. That was Scarlett! Racing past him, with another girl. He mewed hopefully at her, but she'd already disappeared inside the white building.

The door was still open.

Bootle padded out into the empty playground, and hurried over to the door. The noise of the children still echoed around the corridor, and he shivered a little. But if he wanted to find Scarlett, this was where he needed to be. He pattered along the chilly concrete floor, peeping in at the doors when he found an open one. The first classroom he looked into was full of children who were smaller than Scarlett, he thought. A little boy stared at him, and pointed, his eyes widening delightedly. Bootle whisked out of the door as fast as he could. He had a feeling that he wasn't meant to be in here, and he didn't want to be caught before he'd found Scarlett.

The next couple of doors were shut, but then he found one ajar, and looked round it. These children were more the right size. He sidled round the door, and then he saw her, facing away from him, but at the nearest table. The children were all looking away from the door, towards something at the other end of the classroom, so it was easy for Bootle to race across the carpet and hide under the table—right next to Scarlett's feet. He purred quietly to himself. He had done it! He'd found her!

Very gently, he rubbed the side of his head against Scarlett's sock.

Scarlett gave a tiny squeak, and Izzy stared at her. 'What's the matter?'

'Something under the table . . .' Scarlett whispered, her eyes horrified. It was furry. What if it was one of those enormous furry spiders? There were definitely more spiders in the country. She'd found a huge one in the loo at the weekend. Very slowly, she peered under the table, and Izzy looked too.

'A cat!'

'Bootle!'

Mrs Mason looked round sharply, and Izzy and Scarlett tried to look at the board and pretend there wasn't anything under their table.

Bootle purred louder, and patted at Scarlett's leg with a velvety paw.

'What's he doing here?' Izzy whispered, as soon as Mrs Mason had turned back to the board.

'He must have followed us again.' Scarlett was grinning. She couldn't help it. She wasn't quite sure how she was going to sort this out, but she loved it

63

that Bootle wanted to be with her so much that he followed her all the way to school.

Bootle scrambled up on to her lap, and sat there, purring, and nudging at her school cardigan.

Sarah and Millie saw a small ginger head sticking up over the edge of the table, and gasped. Scarlett put a finger to her lips, and stared at them beseechingly. 'Don't tell!' she whispered.

Sarah and Millie shook their heads, to say of course they wouldn't. But Mrs Mason had seen them anyway.

'Scarlett, what's going on?' She came over to their table. 'Oh, it's a kitten. What's he doing here?'

'He followed me from home,' said Scarlett. 'I'm sorry, Mrs Mason. He was under the table, I didn't even know he was here till a minute ago.' She sighed, a very tiny sigh. She'd hoped to keep Bootle a secret for a bit longer.

Mrs Mason smiled. 'Well, he's very sweet, but I'm afraid he can't stay in the classroom. You'd better take him up to the office, and get Mrs Lucy to call home. Is there someone at home who can come and get him?'

Scarlett nodded. 'My dad.' She stood up, with Bootle snuggled against her, and the rest of the class whispered and aahed admiringly, reaching out to stroke him, as she went out of the classroom.

'You're such a star for finding me!' Scarlett whispered, and Bootle purred.

CHAPTER SIX

'I can't believe you followed me all the way, Bootle!' Scarlett told him again, as she cuddled him in between putting her shoes on for school the next day. 'Everybody wanted to know about you. Even people in the year above came to ask who you were—they saw me carrying you up to the office, on their way back from PE.' She sighed, and placed him down on the stairs so she could put on her other shoe. 'But Miss Wilson made Dad promise he wouldn't let it happen again. He said Miss Wilson was really scary. You're going to hate being shut up for the whole day.' She stroked his head, looking at him worriedly. 'I suppose in a few days you'll stop wanting to follow me. But I sort of wish you wouldn't. I love it that you're so clever!'

Bootle clambered up a couple of steps—it took a little while, as his legs were still quite short—so that he could rub his chin on to Scarlett's hair while she did up her shoe. He wasn't sure what she was saying, but it was definitely nice. She was fussing over him, and he liked to be fussed over.

Jackson came stomping down the hallway, and Scarlett turned round and dropped a kiss on the top of Bootle's little furry head. 'I've got to go. Be good, Bootle!'

Bootle sat on the steps and stared at her crossly as she slipped quickly out of the front door, pulling it closed behind her. She had done it again! How many times did he have to follow after them before she decided it would just be easier to take him with them? He jumped down the stairs in two huge leaps, and made for the cat flap at a run. But it was locked. He scrabbled at

it furiously, until Dad came and picked him up.

'Sorry, Bootle. Not happening, little one.'

Bootle wriggled out of his arms, and stalked away across the kitchen. He was going to follow Scarlett—somehow.

He would have to get out of the house a different way. Bootle prowled thoughtfully through the different rooms, sniffing hopefully at the front door to see if it might open. He could smell outside, but the door was very firmly shut. And so were all the windows.

But when Scarlett had taken him upstairs to play the day before, her window had been open. Bootle sat at the bottom of the stairs, and gazed upwards doubtfully. They were very big. But he could do it, if he was careful, and slow.

Determinedly, he began to scrabble and haul himself up, stopping every little while for a rest, until at last he heaved himself on to the landing. His legs felt wobbly, but he made himself keep going, on into Scarlett's room, where the door was open just a crack. As soon as he pushed his way around the door, his ears pricked forward excitedly. The window was open! Just as he had remembered it!

Forgetting how tired his legs were, Bootle sprang up on to the bed, sniffing delightedly at the fresh air blowing in.

The windowsill was too far above the bed for him to reach though. His

whiskers drooped a little. How was he
going to get up there? He padded up
and down the bed and stared at
Scarlett's pile of cuddly toys. She liked
to tease him with them, walking them
up and down the bed for him to pounce
on. But why shouldn't he climb up
them instead? He put out a cautious
paw, testing the back of a fluffy toy cat.

It squashed down a little, but it was still a step up, and then on to the back of a huge teddy, and the stuffed leopard . . . and the windowsill!

Bootle pulled himself up, panting happily as he felt the cool breeze on his whiskers.

Now he only had to get down again on the outside . . .

'No kitten today?' Sarah asked Scarlett, a little sadly.

Scarlett shook her head. 'Miss Wilson made my dad promise he'd keep him in. Poor Bootle. He's going to be so cross.'

'He's the cleverest cat I've ever seen,' Sarah told her admiringly. 'Imagine coming all that way! And he'd never even been to the school before—I don't know how he worked out where to go!'

Scarlett smiled. 'It's amazing, isn't it? I think he must have heard us all in the playground.'

'You ought to stop in at the shop and

buy him a treat on the way home,' Izzy suggested. 'I've got some money, if you haven't any on you.'

Scarlett nodded. 'It's OK, I've got some. That's a really good idea.' She grinned at Izzy. 'You can help me choose.' It was so nice having a friend back for tea—it felt like being back at her old school. Izzy's mum had been fine about her walking back with Scarlett—Izzy usually walked back home too. She had a big sister in Jackson's class.

'He might just about speak to us, if we bring him cat treats . . .'

Bootle scrabbled frantically at the branches of the creeper. It had looked so solid, and easy to climb. But it turned out to be much harder to get down than up. It was also more wobbly, and he didn't like that. The first bit had been easy, just a little jump to that sloping bit of roof, then across the tiles. It was the drop down from the roof that was the problem. His claws were slipping. Bootle gave up trying to cling on, and leaped out, as far away from the wall as he could, hoping that he remembered how to land.

He hit the ground with a jolt, but he was there! In the front garden, right by the gate and the lane. Bootle darted a glance behind him. Then he scrambled under the gate, and set off to find Scarlett, trotting along jauntily. He knew the way now, he didn't have to sniff and search and worry.

He was halfway down the field when it started to rain. A very large drop hit him on the nose, making him shrink back. It was shortly followed by rather a lot of others, and in seconds his fur was plastered flat over his thin ribs. He hid in the hedge, his ears laid back.

He would wait for it to stop, Bootle decided, gazing out disgustedly. He certainly didn't want to go anywhere in that. But it went on, and on, and he needed to find Scarlett. He put his nose out cautiously, and shivered as he felt the drops on his whiskers. It was horrible. But he couldn't stay here all day . . .

At last he slunk out from under the hedge, plodding through the wet muddy ruts, and hoping that Scarlett would have something warm and dry to rub him with when he got to the school. He scurried down the pavement, through the puddles, so miserable that he didn't even bother to dart into the hedge to avoid the car going past. The driver of the car didn't see the soaked little kitten, and even if he had, he probably wouldn't have been able to avoid the huge puddle that splashed up over Bootle like a wave. There was so much water that he staggered back, letting out a mew of cold and dismay.

Then he flat out ran for the school, racing across the playground towards that lovely, warm, open door.

But it was closed.

It had been wet play, and no one had wanted the rain blowing in. All the doors were closed, every single one— as the soaked, mouse-brown-striped kitten found when he ran frantically all the way round the building.

Remembering the window he had climbed out of at home, Bootle looked up to see if there were any he could get through. There was a bench up against the wall, with a window right above it, and he jumped for the seat, scrabbling desperately until he could heave himself up. Then it was a little hop on to the arm, and then again on to the windowsill. But the window was shut, and everyone was gathered together at the other end of the classroom, looking at something and talking excitedly. They didn't hear him scratching hopefully at the window, and at last he jumped down.

Bootle sat under the bench and mewed miserably, calling for someone

to come and let him in. He didn't care
if they took him back to the cottage
again, as long as he was out of the rain.
He would stay at home, and never try
to follow anyone, if only he was dry.

No one came. No one heard him
over the hammering and splashing of
the rain, and the bench was dripping all
over him. Bootle crawled out, looking

around for another place to shelter. There were trees, over on the edge of the path to the field. Perhaps it would be drier there. He ran through the wet grass, shivering as the stems rubbed along his soaked fur, and shaking water drops off his whiskers. He was so cold. Sitting still under the bench had made him shiver, and now he couldn't stop.

Then something made his ears flick up a little. There was another building. Just a little one, a shed, and he could see that the door was open!

Bootle made one last effort, forcing his shaky paws to race to the shed, and struggle over the step and into the dusty dryness. He was so relieved to be out of the rain that he hardly noticed the sports equipment piled up all over the place—just the heap of old, rather tattered mats that he could curl up on for a rest.

It was while Bootle was fast asleep that the caretaker remembered he hadn't locked up the shed when he'd got out the spare chairs, and came grumpily back through the rain with his keys.

CHAPTER SEVEN

'Bootle!' Scarlett called happily, as she opened the front door to let herself and Izzy and Jackson inside. 'Bootle, come and see Izzy!'

Dad hurried out of the kitchen, a worried expression on his face. 'You didn't see him in the lane then?'

Scarlett stared at him, not understanding. 'What?' she asked, with a frown.

'Bootle! He's not out there? I wondered if he'd slipped out somehow. He must have done, I can't find him anywhere.' Dad glanced distractedly up and down the hallway, as though he thought Bootle might pop out from behind the wellies.

'You can't find him?' Scarlett stammered. 'You mean—he's lost?'

'I'm sorry, Scarlett.' Dad ran his fingers through his hair till it stood up on end. 'I had a long phone meeting all morning, it finished about an hour ago. Then I went to find Bootle and check that he was all right, but he'd disappeared. I just don't understand how he can have got out!'

'Maybe he didn't?' Izzy suggested shyly. 'He could be shut in somewhere. Olly's always doing that. He climbed into a drawer once and went to sleep, and my mum didn't see him and she shut the drawer. Then she got a real shock because her wardrobe was meowing.'

'Maybe . . .' Dad murmured. But he looked doubtful. 'Let's check again.'

Scarlett grabbed Izzy's hand and pulled her up the stairs, while Jackson hurried into the living room.

'Bathroom,' Scarlett muttered. 'Not in here. The airing cupboard, maybe?' She pulled the door open, but no

80

indignant kitten darted out. 'Jackson's room . . .' She peered in, and called, 'Bootle! Bootle! He isn't here, Izzy. I'm sure he'd come if he heard me calling. Or he'd meow to tell me where he was.'

'He could be asleep. Try the other rooms, just in case.'

Scarlett peered into her mum and dad's room, opening the wardrobe, and all the drawers, but there weren't even any gingery hairs. 'This is my room,' she told Izzy, pushing the last door open. 'Bootle!' Scarlett caught her breath. She'd been hoping to find him asleep on her bed, but he wasn't there.

'Your window's open . . .' Izzy said slowly.

'Oh, but he couldn't get out through that.' Scarlett shook her head. 'It's really high.'

Izzy frowned. 'It depends how much he wanted to.'

The girls climbed on to the bed so they could look out of the window.

'You see? He could jump on there.' Izzy pointed out the low bit of the roof. 'And there's all that ivy stuff. That's like a cat ladder.'

Scarlett stared at her. 'You think he really could have climbed down that?'

Izzy looked down at the grass, which was an awfully long way away. 'He might have done.'

Dad came in, with Jackson behind. 'He isn't in the house,' he said grimly. 'Was that window open, Scarlett?'

'Yes!' Scarlett nodded, her eyes filling with tears. 'I'm really sorry, Dad, I didn't think Bootle would try to climb out of it! He can hardly get up the stairs, and the windowsill's really high.'

'It isn't your fault.' Dad put an arm round her. 'I should have checked on him earlier. None of us realized he would be able to climb out of the window.' He leaned over to look out. 'I think he did, though. Some of that creeper's been torn away.'

'Can we go and look for him?' Scarlett asked. 'He might have tried to get to school again, and got lost . . . Oh, Dad, what if he's gone on the road?'

Dad hugged her tighter. 'Don't panic, Scarlett. I don't think he would, he's scared of the car noises. Remember how he meowed when we got him out of the car at the vet's? Even though he was safe in his basket he didn't like it when the cars went past. And why would he get mixed up about the way to school, when he made it yesterday?' He let go of Scarlett, and made for the door. 'I'm just going to call the school and see if he's turned up there.'

Scarlett sank down on her bed, staring up at Izzy. 'I can't believe it. Everyone's been telling me today how lucky I am, and how gorgeous Bootle is, and now he's gone. I've only had him a couple of weeks, Izzy! How can I have lost him?'

It was starting to get dark. Bootle scratched at the door with his claws again, but they were starting to hurt. He'd hoped that he could make that little thin strip of light and fresh air bigger, maybe even big enough to squeeze out. But all he'd managed to do was scratch off some of the paint. Miserably, he sank down, mewing faintly. No one seemed to hear him, and it had been quite a while since he'd last heard anyone outside.

Maybe he would have to stay here all night, he thought anxiously. Scarlett wouldn't know where he was. Perhaps she was looking for him? He stood up again quickly, even though his paws felt sore, and meowed as loud as he could. Scarlett would look for him, he was sure of it.

But even though he called and called and called to her, she didn't come, and at last he had to give up. He was worn out with scratching and meowing, and he dragged his sore paws back to the pile of mats. Then he curled up into a tight little ball, and lay there in the gathering darkness, wondering how long it would be before anyone found him.

'We can make some "lost" posters,' Izzy suggested the next morning. 'If we ask Mrs Mason nicely, I bet she'll let us use the ICT suite. We could put them up all round the village on the way home.'

Scarlett nodded. She should have thought of that the night before. After Izzy had gone home, she and Jackson had searched the house all over again, and then Scarlett had gone to bed, and cried herself to sleep, knowing that her little kitten wasn't curled up in his basket in the kitchen—he was out there in the dark, and she had no idea where.

'We could go round the houses between here and school, and ask if anyone's seen him,' she suggested, shivering at the thought of poor Bootle wandering around lost somewhere.

'Ooh, yes,' Izzy agreed. 'We could get people to check their garages. Don't worry, Scarlett, I can help with that. I know almost everybody in the village, and it's scary if you don't know people.'

'That would be great,' Scarlett said. She'd do anything if it meant finding Bootle, even if she had to talk to hundreds of grumpy people.

A couple of the Year Six girls came past Scarlett and Izzy on their way in. 'Hey, Scarlett! Did you get into trouble with Miss Wilson yesterday?' one of them asked.

Scarlett stared at her in bewilderment. 'W-what?' she murmured, suddenly shy.

'When your kitten came back! I thought your brother said Miss Wilson had told your dad off? That he had to keep your kitten at home?'

Scarlett forgot all about being shy. 'You mean you saw Bootle? Are you sure it was yesterday?' she asked the older girl eagerly.

'Yeah, definitely . . .' The older girl— Scarlett was pretty sure she was called Eleanor—frowned. 'I saw him looking in the classroom window, but then he ran off. Why? What's the matter?'

'Bootle's lost,' Scarlett explained. 'Dad had him shut in, but he climbed out of an upstairs window. We think he must have tried to follow us. We weren't sure he had made it to school, but if you saw him, then he was definitely here!'

'You're not mixing up the days?' Izzy asked Eleanor doubtfully.

Eleanor shook her head. 'Nope. I'm certain. It was yesterday when it was raining. And your kitten was soaked, Scarlett. His fur was actually dripping. I saw him out of the window; he was in the playground. Before break, I think.'

'He must have got out of the window really soon after we left,' Scarlett murmured. 'Thank you, Eleanor! I have to go and look for him!'

CHAPTER EIGHT

There was sunlight coming in from somewhere else, Bootle noticed, as the shed grew slowly lighter that morning. It wasn't just the space around the door. Where there was light, perhaps there was some sort of hole, or another window that might be open, so he could climb through it.

It was up at the top, near the ceiling, he thought. Very high up. Much higher than Scarlett's window. But then, there were a lot more things to climb in here. Piles of chairs, some benches and more of those mats. He'd just have to find a way to reach it.

Bootle was sure that Scarlett was looking for him—almost sure, anyway. But the shed was all the way across the field from the school, he'd realized, as he lay curled up on the mats. What if Scarlett didn't know about it? He couldn't wait for someone to let him out. He would have to do it for himself.

He stretched out his paws, which felt a little better this morning, though they still ached from all that scrabbling and scratching. Then he padded across the pile of mats, and made a wobbly jump on to an old wooden bench. That was the first step . . .

'Where do we start?' Izzy asked, as they hurried across the playground.

'I don't know. Maybe we should find Jackson and tell him that those girls saw Bootle,' Scarlett suggested, but she couldn't see her brother anywhere, and she wanted to get started searching. 'My dad rang up yesterday, remember? And he spoke to Mrs Lucy in the office, and she went and asked in the staff room. No one had seen Bootle. So he wasn't just hanging around school looking for us.'

Izzy frowned. 'I know I keep going on about him being shut in somewhere, but . . .'

Scarlett shook her head. 'No, I think you're right! It's the only thing that makes sense. But where?'

Izzy shook her head. 'I don't know. Maybe the classroom cupboards? Do you think if we asked Mrs Lucy we could go and look? Oh no! There's the bell.'

Scarlett looked anxiously round as everyone began to collect their stuff and head into school. 'I can't go into school now! I can't! Bootle's here somewhere, I know he is!'

Izzy patted her shoulder. 'It's OK. Look, we'll tell Mrs Mason that Bootle might be here. We have to go in, Scarlett. We'll get in trouble otherwise.'

Scarlett almost didn't care, but she supposed Izzy was right. Maybe they could ask the head teacher what to do? She'd said her dog used to follow her to school. She'd understand.

But Miss Wilson was talking to one of the other teachers, and she just waved the girls past when Scarlett tried to hover in the doorway and talk to her.

Mrs Mason was late coming into their class, and when she finally arrived she had her arms full of different coloured PE bibs, and she didn't look as though she wanted to hear about kittens, even though Izzy tried her best.

'Oh dear . . . Well, I'm sure you can have a look at break,' she said distractedly, when the girls tried to explain. 'Sit down, please, you two.'

Sit down! Scarlett opened her mouth to argue, but Mrs Mason wasn't even looking at her any more.

'Once we've done the register, everyone, I've got some exciting news—we're going to start practising for Sports Day. We've scheduled in a couple of extra PE sessions, and the first one is this morning. So let's just mark everyone in . . .' She moved names around on the whiteboard. 'Where's Keisha? Is she still not well? OK.'

'I don't want to do PE,' Scarlett whispered frantically. 'I have to go and look for Bootle!'

'PE!' Izzy nudged her. 'I've just thought! Shut up in a shed, Scarlett, we said he might be!'

'What are you talking about?' Scarlett was biting back tears.

'There's a little shed at the end of the field, where Mr Larkin, the caretaker, keeps stuff that doesn't get used all that much. He was definitely carrying

chairs in and out yesterday; I heard him complaining about how wet he'd got.'

'So the shed was open?' Scarlett breathed, her eyes widening.

Izzy nodded. 'It must have been.'

'Now go and get changed, please, everyone,' Mrs Mason called. 'Then we'll go up to the hall, as it's still a bit too wet on the field.'

'I'm not getting changed,' Scarlett said, glaring at Izzy as though she thought her friend might tell her off. 'I'm going to find Bootle.'

Izzy shrugged. 'Uh-huh, and I'm coming with you. Come on.'

They hurried out of the classroom, ahead of everyone else, and Izzy grabbed Scarlett's hand. 'It's this way. There's a side door, come on.' She pulled Scarlett down the corridor, and pushed open a door Scarlett hadn't even known about. 'Quick way out to the field.'

'Hey, Izzy!' someone called. 'We're in the hall, not the field! And you aren't changed!'

But Izzy and Scarlett were already

running across the damp grass.

Bootle wobbled on the old chair. He was almost there—he could see the narrow wooden windowsill and the dirty pane of glass. The wind was shaking it, as though it was loose. If he could only get to it, maybe he could push his way out, somehow?

He balanced himself again, teetering on the edge of the chair. He'd scrambled his way up the whole pile, and it had taken so long. If he misjudged his jump to the window, he wasn't sure he'd have the strength to climb up all over again. He was so hungry, and tired, and his paws hurt.

His whiskers flicked and shook as he tried to work out how he could make the jump. It was much further than he'd ever jumped before. And the strip of wood along the window was so very small. But if it meant he could get out . . . Then he would go back home, and wait there for Scarlett. He would see if he could get back in through the cat flap.

He tensed his muscles to spring, and crouched there, trembling a little, trying to summon up the courage to leap.

Then his ears twitched. He could hear someone! People, talking!

'Bootle! Bootle, are you in there? Is the door locked, Izzy?'

That was Scarlett!

Bootle let out a shrill desperate meow, and forgot to worry about how narrow the ledge was. He just went for it, scrabbling madly with his paws as he almost made it, and then heaving himself up on to the windowsill.

Then he batted his paws against the glass, mewing frantically.

'I can hear him! He is in there, Izzy, you were right!'

'It's locked. I'll go and get Mr Larkin.'

Bootle heard feet thudding away, and cried out in panic. They hadn't heard him! They were going!

'It's OK, Bootle. Where are you?'

There were noises outside and Bootle banged his nose against the grubby window, trying to see what was happening.

Scarlett pulled herself up onto the little tiny ledge on the outside of the window. 'I can see you! It's really you, Bootle. Oh, I've been so worried. I can't believe you climbed out of a window.' She giggled with relief, and sniffed. 'And now you're trying to climb out of this one, aren't you, silly kitten.'

Bootle mewed and scraped, but the window wouldn't open. How was he going to get to Scarlett?

'Oh! Mr Larkin! The keys!' Scarlett's face disappeared from the window, and Bootle wriggled himself round as the door rattled and shook. And then it opened.

With a joyful yowl, he bounded back to the wobbly chair, and took a flying leap to the mats, and then Scarlett was there, hugging him.

Bootle purred and purred, and rubbed his face against hers, and purred louder.

'Izzy! Scarlett! What are you doing out here? Oh! Oh, no, has he been shut in here?' Mrs Mason peered worriedly into the dusty shed.

'All night,' Scarlett told her, shivering. 'Can I call my dad, Mrs Mason, please? Can I take him home?'

Mrs Mason nodded. 'Yes, you'd better take him up to the office again. I hope he doesn't keep doing this, Scarlett.'

Scarlett stroked Bootle, who was pressed against her cardigan like he never meant to let go. 'Me too.'

'Well, he got soaking wet and trapped in a shed, so maybe he'll stay at home now,' Izzy suggested.

Scarlett nodded. 'He looks like he wants to go home,' she agreed, feeling the sharp little points of Bootle's claws hooked into her cardigan. 'I promise I won't ever let you get lost again,' she whispered to him, feeling his whiskers brush across her cheek. 'I'll look after you always.'

'I'm really glad my mum said I could come back with you.' Izzy sighed happily and blew on her hot chocolate.

Scarlett nodded, stroking Bootle, who was curled up on her lap, with his claws hooked determinedly into her school skirt. He wasn't letting her go. 'We might never have worked out where he was if it wasn't for you! He could have been stuck in there for ages—until Mr Larkin had to put the chairs away again.'

Bootle purred as Scarlett gently rubbed behind his ears. He was finally starting to feel properly warm again.

Scarlett's dad had lit the fire in the living room, and the girls were huddled in front of it—it was raining again, so it had been a wet walk home. They'd splashed through the puddles as fast as they could, anxious to see Bootle again, and check that he was OK.

'Do you want any more hot chocolate, girls?' Dad asked. 'Jackson's after another cup.'

Scarlett shook her head. 'No, thanks.'

Izzy smiled at him. 'No, that's OK, thanks. It was lovely. It's a pity cats can't have hot drinks, though, Bootle must have been frozen after a night in the shed.'

'I've had him on my lap ever since I picked him up,' Dad told them. 'Apart from when he was wolfing down a massive dinner and breakfast in one. He definitely wanted company, and since he couldn't have you, Scarlett, I was the next best thing.'

'I hope he's not going to follow us again tomorrow,' Scarlett said, looking down at him anxiously. He didn't look very adventurous at the moment . . .

Dad shook his head. 'No, I'm sure

he'll remember being trapped. He won't want that to happen again. But I promise I will make sure every window's closed. I'll even let him play with the computer, Scarlett.' He grinned. 'I'll find him one of those homework websites, then he won't need to go to school.'

Bootle stretched out his paws and stared up at them in surprise as they laughed, and then he huddled himself back into the front of Scarlett's cardigan. It was lovely and warm inside. And dry. He hadn't realized how damp and miserable it could be, following people. For the moment, he was going to stay right here.